You go to school every day.

So does Patrick.

Maybe you ride on a schoolbus.

So does Patrick.

After school you play with your friends.

So does Patrick.

In fact, there's only one difference between you and Patrick.

But it is a *big* difference.

Patrick is a dinosaur. A *big* dinosaur.

Patrick's friends are dinosaurs, too.

So is his teacher.

So are his Mom and Dad.

What's it like to be a student in a school for dinosaurs?

That's what Dino School is all about!

Look for all of the fun DINO SCHOOL books:

#1 *A Puzzle for Apatosaurus*—on sale now.
#2 *Halloween Double Dare*
#3 *Battle of the Class Clowns*—coming in
    November.
#4 *Sneeze-o-saurus*—coming in December.

Don't miss these other exciting series from HARPER PAPERBACKS FOR KIDS:

VIC THE VAMPIRE
What do you do when your best friend is a vampire?

#1 *School Ghoul*—on sale now.
#2 *Science Spook*—on sale now.

THE KIDS ON THE BUS
For kids who ride the bus—and those who wish they did!

#1 *School Bus Cat*—coming in November.

HALLOWEEN
DOUBLE DARE

Jacqueline A. Ball
Illustrated by David Schulz

Harper Paperbacks

Harper & Row, Publishers, New York
Grand Rapids, Philadelphia, St. Louis, San Francisco
London, Singapore, Sydney, Tokyo, Toronto

For John and Ashley, with love

Special thanks to my talented creative writing students in the Center School GRASP Program, Old Lyme, Connecticut: Amy, Charlie, Emily, Kristo, Kyra, Marc, and Zack.

Harper Paperbacks a division of Harper & Row. Publishers, Inc.
10 East 53rd Street, New York, N.Y. 10022

Copyright © 1990 by Jacqueline A. Ball

Produced by Jacqueline A. Ball Associates, Inc.

Cover and interior design by Nancy Norton, Norton & Company

First printing: October, 1990

Printed in the United States of America

HARPER PAPERBACKS and colophon are trademarks of Harper & Row, Publishers, Inc.

10 9 8 7 6 5 4 3 2 1

CHAPTER
1

It was the Saturday afternoon before Halloween. Sara and Ty Triceratops were raking leaves.

They had already raked two neat piles in the backyard. Now there were two more in the front.

"Super job, twins," Mom would say.

Sara smiled. She liked doing a good job. Of course, she'd rather do a good job solving mysteries. That was her favorite thing to do.

Suddenly Sara felt the ground shake.

"What was that?" she called to Ty.

A few leaves drifted out of the piles.

"Maybe an earthquake!" he cried.

The ground shook some more.

Sara peered over the fence.

"That's no earthquake," Sara said. "It's just our friends. I wonder why they're in such a hurry."

Three young dinosaurs were running down the street. They glanced over their shoulders as they ran.

Annette Anatosaurus was the first through the front gate. Annette was the fastest runner in Dino School. She was also Sara's best friend.

"He's right behind us!" she yelled.

Annette raced past the twins.

The breeze almost blew the bows off Sara's horns.

More leaves flew out of the piles.

"*Who's* right behind you?" called Ty.

But Annette was gone.

Patrick Apatosaurus came next.

"Boy, is he mad!" Patrick cried.

Sara thought Patrick was the nicest

dino in their class. He was so gentle and cheerful.

He was also big. He made a gigantic draft.

Whoosh. Sara and Ty were flattened back against the fence.

The leaf piles became leaf tornadoes.

"Who's mad, Patrick?" Sara yelled.

But Patrick was gone, too.

The third dino jogged into the yard. He wore sunglasses and a jean jacket.

"Man, that dude is steamed," he said.

It was Stanley Stegosaurus, better known as Spike. He was Patrick's best friend.

Spike didn't look as worried as the others. Spike never looked worried. He always looked cool, with his shades and his terrific clothes. They were a special brand. Dino-Dude Duds.

Spike's spiked tail dragged through

what was left of the neat piles. Sara and Ty groaned.

"Oops, sorry, guys," Spike apologized.

"That's okay," said Ty. "Just *please* tell us who you're running away from."

"Well, I'll give you a hint," Spike answered. "I'll even give you three hints. Big, bad, bully."

Sara made a face. "Rex."

Tyrannosaurus Rex was the meanest dino around.

He tore the training wheels off little dinos' bikes.

He stole smart dinos' homework.

He ran down skateboarders with his big black bike.

Rex *loved* being bad.

"What's he doing around here?" asked Sara.

"I guess he followed us from McDino's," Spike said. "We were all getting some French fries. We didn't see him, but I know he hangs out there."

The dinos ran to the backyard.

"Annette dared us to go to Fossil Street," Spike continued. "That's where we—um—ran into Rex."

The dinos loved to play Double Dare. One dino would dare another to sing extra loud in chorus. Or to run the bases backward in gym.

The next one would dare another to put a smelly sneaker in a locker. Dino sneakers could really smell.

Annette usually started it.

"Fossil Street!" Sara exclaimed.

"Yeah," Spike said. "Where Mr. Trachodon lives."

"I've heard a witch lives there, too," said Ty. "She laughs all night."

Ty made his voice high and cackly.

"He-he-he-he-HE!"

Sara shivered. "I've heard there are always weird shadows in the window," she said. "And every Halloween Mr. Trachodon drags a big sack into the house. Then he drags it out the next night and puts it with the garbage."

She paused. "A sack big enough to hold a dino!"

The dinos were behind the house now. Suddenly they forgot about Mr. Trachodon and started to laugh.

Patrick and Annette were behind an apple tree. They were trying to hide. But the tree wasn't big enough.

Patrick's neck hung over a branch.

Annette's tail stuck out on one side.

"What's so funny?" Patrick asked.

"You," Ty answered. "You haven't picked a very good hiding place."

Sara glanced around. "Let's hide

behind the shed in the side yard."

They tumbled across the lawn. They crouched behind an old shed.

"Okay, finish your story about Fossil Street," Ty said to Spike.

"Annette dared us to walk past Mr. Trachodon's house. So we did."

"That was really brave!" exclaimed Sara. She gave Patrick a big smile.

He turned bright red. Patrick was shy around girls. Especially Sara. He knew she liked him.

"Then we dared her to knock on the door."

"So I did," said Annette. "But no one answered."

"*Then* Annette dared Patrick to ring the doorbell," Spike said.

"That's what I was just about to do," Patrick explained, "when I ran into Rex. I was across the street, getting a running start. I guess I had my eyes closed. I didn't see Rex coming. We crashed into each other."

"Some of the spokes on his bike got bent," said Annette.

"Which is why *he's* bent out of shape," finished Spike. "You know how he loves that bike."

They heard a loud whirring sound. Then they heard tires squealing.

"Speak of the dino-devil," said Ty.

The dinos peeked around the building.

Rex was at the gate. He sat on a big black bike.

He was reading the mailbox.

Suddenly he looked up. A grin full of sharp, jagged teeth filled his face.

"Yoo-hoo, Ty and Sara," he called in a pretend friendly voice. "Can you come out and play?"

No one said a word.

Rex walked his bike inside the gate. Then he pushed it across the grass. He was almost at the shed!

The dinos crouched down lower.

Just then they heard a wonderful sound. It was a mom's voice.

"Sara! Ty! Where are you?"

"Saved by the mom!" Sara said.

They peeked out at Rex. He was snarling.

"I guess he heard her, too," said Patrick. "Whew!"

Rex shook a big fist at the shed.

Then he picked up one of the rakes. He threw it as high as he could.

It stuck in a willow tree.

"Creep!" Ty muttered.

Then Rex saw a soccer ball on the grass. He took a running jump and kicked it as hard as he could. The other dinos watched as all the air flowed out.

"I guess we won't be playing soccer today," Annette said.

Rex still wasn't finished. He got on his bike.

He took careful aim.

Smack! Splat! Leaves sprayed out everywhere. Now all four piles were completely destroyed.

"Oh, no!" Sara cried. A whole afternoon's work!

Rex rode off down the street.

Mrs. Triceratops came out of the house with a big basket.

"Hi, everyone. What are you up to?"

"Er, nothing, Mom," Ty said.

"Well, how about getting me some apples?" Mrs. Triceratops asked. "I want to make some pies for dessert."

"Sure, Mom," said Sara. She took the basket.

Mrs. Triceratops looked across the lawn. Her forehead wrinkled up. "Why, those leaves look awfully sloppy, twins. You two usually do such a good job."

Sara was furious. That Rex!

"We'll fix them, Mom," Ty promised.

"All right, but hurry. It will be dark soon."

She went back into the house.

"Hi-ho, hi-ho, it's back to work we go," sang Ty. "Patrick, give me a hand, okay?"

"You mean, give you a neck," corrected Spike.

"Whatever," Ty said. He jumped on Patrick's neck. Patrick moved toward the willow tree. Now Ty could reach way up.

Ty shook a branch. The rake came tumbling down.

He slid down Patrick's neck.

"I'll get the apples too," said Patrick. He walked over and gently nudged the apple tree with his head.

Ripe red apples bounced down.

Sara caught most of them in the basket.

Spike caught a couple on his tail. He juggled them a few times. Then he cored them with his spikes. "Anyone for a snack?"

The dinos ate apples and raked leaves for a while.

"I'm so mad at that bully Rex!" Sara said. "Someone should teach him a lesson."

Spike swept the leaves into a bag with his tail.

"Yeah," he agreed. "Someone should. But we've got more important things to talk about now. Like Halloween."

"Right," said Annette eagerly. "We

13

have to get our costumes ready. The contest is next week."

"What are you going to be, Sara?" Patrick asked shyly.

"A fairy princess," she answered. "With a long pink cloak."

"I'm going to be a lion," said Ty. "Then I can roar right up to Rex and scare him silly." He made a low growl. "AAAARRL!"

"I think I'm going to be Len Lambeosaurus," Patrick told them. "He's the pitcher for the Denver Dinos. I already have a Denver Dinos hat."

He reached up to pat the baseball cap that he always wore. It wasn't there!

"My hat!" he cried. "I must have dropped it—back on Fossil Street!"

CHAPTER
2

Patrick looked like he was trying not to cry. Sara knew how much he loved his baseball cap.

"Don't worry," she told him. "We'll get it back."

"But it's almost dark. Fossil Street is scary even in the daylight!"

"Oh, Patrick, you're such a chicken," Annette teased.

"I am not!"

Annette folded her arms. "Then prove it. I *dare* you to go back."

Patrick didn't say anything.

Neither did anyone else.

"We *should* get it now," Ty finally agreed. "If we wait until tomorrow, it might not be there."

"I'll help you, buddy," Spike told his friend. He turned to Annette. "And afterwards, *we* get to dare *you*!"

She shrugged. "Fine with me!"

"Well, what are we waiting for?" asked Sara. She tried to sound brave. For Patrick's sake.

The sunlight was fading as they walked the few blocks to Fossil Street.

The air was getting colder, too.

Sara's teeth were chattering.

The dinos turned off Lizard Lane. Then they were on Fossil Street. There were only three or four houses on the street, with empty lots in between. The houses were run-down. The empty lots were full of weeds.

They stopped near one of the lots.

They could see Mr. Trachodon's house clearly.

It was the scariest-looking house on the street.

Its gray paint was peeling. Its front porch was sagging. Shingles were missing from the roof. Shades hung crookedly in all the windows.

A raggedy hedge surrounded the house.

A Denver Dinos cap was lying on the hedge.

"Lucky us," Spike whispered. "It's still there."

"We'll watch in case you get in trouble," said Sara.

Spike and Patrick walked slowly down the street.

They looked to the right. They looked to the left. They dashed past the house. As they did, Patrick whipped his tail up against the hedge.

The cap flew off.

Spike caught it with *his* tail.

Then the two spun around and raced back to their friends.

"What a team!" exclaimed Sara.

"All right!" cried Ty.

"Not bad," admitted Annette.

Spike and Patrick slapped hands. Patrick was beaming with happiness. He pulled the cap down onto his head.

"Let's go," he said. "My mom will be worried."

"Besides, it's suppertime," said Ty. "I could eat a cow!"

"Euw, gross," said Annette. "That's what Rex eats."

"Speaking of Rex," Sara said, "we have to think of a way to get him back."

"Speaking of what Rex eats," said Spike, "I have an idea for a dare."

He whispered something to Patrick. Patrick whispered to Ty.

Ty whispered to Sara.

Annette tapped her foot.

"We dare you to steal Rex's lunch, Annette," Spike finally said.

"On Monday," Patrick continued.

"Then switch it with something he'll hate," finished Sara. "That will really show him!"

Annette looked bored. "Big deal," she said. "I'm not scared of Rex."

"Ha!" cried Ty. "You ran away from him as fast as anyone else."

"*Faster* then anyone else," corrected Spike.

Annette tossed her head. "So what? It wasn't because I was scared. If you don't believe me, just wait until Monday. You'll see!"

Her voice trailed off. She was staring at Mr. Trachodon's house.

The other dinos looked, too.

They saw a dim light shining through the front window's shade.

Then they saw shadows! Swooping, leaping shadows on the shade! Monster shadows. Witch shadows.

"He-he-he-HE!!! He-he-he-HE!"

Someone was screaming with laughter! High, witchy laughter!

"Run!" they all yelled at once.

They raced all the way to Sara and Ty's house.

Sara leaned against the front gate. She was panting.

"Let's *never* go to Fossil Street again. No matter what!"

CHAPTER

3

Monday morning was sunny and warm. Groups of dinos were playing outside Dino School before the bell.

Patrick and Ty were looking at some of Patrick's baseball cards. He had hundreds of them in his collection.

Spike and Hank Ankylosaur were playing Heads and Tailsies on the field. Hank's nickname was Hank the Tank. He was the funniest dino in the third grade.

Hank banged a big rubber ball over a net with his tail. His tail had a thick club on the end of it.

Spike bounced the ball off the pointy plates on his head and neck. It sailed back to Hank.

The other dinos had already told Hank about their scary time on Fossil Street. Now Spike was telling him about the dare.

"See, first Annette messes up Rex's lunch," he said.

"Yeah, with something really gross," Patrick called.

"Then Annette gets to dare someone else," finished Ty.

"If she lives that long," added Hank.

He launched the ball way, way up above the playground.

The bell rang.

The ball came down. Spike bounced it around on his back. Then he caught it between his spikes.

"Let's finish up later, okay?" he asked.

"You're on," Hank agreed. "Tie score: five hundred to five hundred."

They had been playing every day

since school started.

Inside, the halls were decorated for Halloween. Rows of dino skeletons were pinned along the tops of the bulletin boards. Rows of pumpkins were on the bottom. The poems in the Poetry Corner were about Halloween.

A big cardboard ghost was taped to the door of Room 211. It said, "Whooooooooooose Room Is this?"

All their names were written on the ghost. They had made their writing spooky and used black crayon.

Their teacher was standing at the door. She smiled as they came in.

Her name was Mrs. Diplodocus. The dinos called her Mrs. D.

Mrs. D. was very tall. She had a long, long neck. She liked to wear lots of necklaces on it.

Today she was wearing six. Three

had green beads. Three had white.

They looked pretty with her greenish-blue skin.

"Good morning," she said. "Isn't it a lovely day?"

The boys saw Sara at the pencil sharpener. She was telling Maggie Megalosaurus and Diana Deinonychus about the dare.

"Annette's going to mess up his *lunch*?" Maggie asked. She looked shocked. Maggie loved to eat.

She clutched a giant laundry bag. Sara knew it was full of sandwiches and candy bars. Maybe bags of potato chips, too.

"She'd better not touch mine!" Maggie said.

"Where *is* Annette, anyway?" asked Diana. She spoke in a tiny little voice. Diana was the smallest dino in the class. "I don't see her."

Annette came rushing in. She was carrying a big brown supermarket bag. Her eyes glowed with excitement.

The dino friends surrounded her.

"Do you have it?" asked Sara.

"Where is it?" asked Ty.

"What is it?" asked Patrick.

"Do you think there'll be any leftovers?" asked Maggie.

Swish-thump. Swish-thump.

Mrs. D. was tapping her tail. That meant she wanted quiet.

Annette whispered to the others.

Swish-thump!

They all sat down.

"Rex isn't here," Annette said to Sara. Their desks were pushed together so they faced each other.

"He's always late," Sara replied. "He'll show up."

Mrs. D. was writing on the board. "I know you've all been working hard on your costumes," she said. "You probably don't need a reminder, but . . ."

She moved so they could see.

TOMORROW
HALLOWEEN COSTUME CONTEST
TWO O'CLOCK IN THE AUDITORIUM

Every year at Dino School there were different Halloween projects. This year the fifth graders got to paint scary pictures on their classroom windows. The fourth grade classes had acted out a scary play. The whole school had watched it last week.

Now Mrs. D's class and Mr. Pterodactyl's class were having a costume contest.

Patrick raised his hand. "Are you going to wear a costume, too?" he

27

asked shyly.

Mrs. D. winked one big green eye. "Who knows?"

She wrote on the board again.

PRIZES FOR

MOST ORIGINAL   FUNNIEST

PRETTIEST   SCARIEST

"You'll get it for prettiest," Annette told Sara. "Your princess costume sounds gorgeous!"

"Leave your costumes behind the stage tomorrow," reminded Mrs. D.

Just then the windows started to rattle. A book slid off a shelf.

Ty turned to Sara and Annette.

"Here comes Rex. On the run."

Rex stormed into the classroom.

He carried a brown bag just like Annette's. It was just like the ones he carried every day.

The dinos knew it held a dozen roast

beef sandwiches. He hated everything but meat. Especially vegetables.

Wimp food, he called them.

Mrs. D's voice was calm. "Sit down, Rex. And *please* try to be on time."

Rex glared at everyone. He stared hardest at the dinos who had been at Sara and Ty's on Saturday. Then he stomped to his seat.

Along the way he stepped on Ty's foot.

"Hey!" Ty protested.

He pulled one of Sara's horns.

"Ouch!" she yelped.

Rex flopped into his seat. Mrs. D. was writing on the board again. She hadn't seen a thing.

"Remember the plan," Annette whispered.

"Don't worry," Sara answered. Her horn was smarting. "Just say when."

CHAPTER
4

First the class took a spelling test.

"These are the words we had last Monday," said Mrs. D. "You've had a whole week to work on them."

She read from a list. "Extra. Extreme."

"These aren't so hard," Annette whispered.

"Extinct."

"I hate that one," complained Sara. "I never get it right."

Then it was time for math problems.

"The Tarbosaurus family eats 4,000 pounds of food a day," said Mrs. D. "How many tons of food do they have to buy every week?"

"Depends on if Maggie comes over," muttered Hank.

It seemed like the morning would never end!

Everyone kept trying not to look at Rex.

Everyone kept glancing at Annette. Would she lose her nerve?

Annette kept looking at the clock.

Finally she took out a plain piece of paper. In big block letters she wrote: SOMEONE STOLE YOUR BIKE.

She folded the note in half. REX, she wrote on it.

Annette passed the note to Sara. Sara passed it to Spike. Spike passed it to Hank. Hank passed it to little Diana. She sat right behind Rex.

Diana slipped it onto the floor behind Rex's foot. She was so tiny and quick he didn't even notice.

"Lunchtime!" called Mrs. D.

Rex jumped up. His foot connected with the note. He picked it up and unfolded it.

Spike, Hank, Ty, and Patrick moved slowly toward the door. They stole glances at Rex.

Suddenly Rex threw back his head and howled. "NOOOOO!"

Then he zoomed out of the room.

Mrs. D. stared at the empty doorway. "What happened?"

"I guess Rex was hungrier than usual," Hank explained.

Their teacher shook her head. She pointed at the bag on Rex's desk. "But he didn't take his lunch. I'm sure he'll be back. I'll wait for him."

The dinos started to leave. Annette got behind Patrick as they passed Rex's desk. Now Mrs. D. couldn't see her.

She grabbed Rex's lunch bag and put a different bag on the desk.

Smiling sweetly at their teacher, the dinos walked into the hall. Then they bent over double, laughing.

"I can't wait to see how Rex likes his new diet," Annette said. She threw his real lunch in a trash can.

"Oh, don't do that!" Maggie exclaimed. She pulled it back out. "For later," she said happily.

"You didn't give him anything that would make him sick, did you?" Patrick asked. He sounded worried.

"No, don't worry. It's all good, healthy stuff," Annette told Patrick. "Just what he hates the most."

"Let's go," said Spike. Sandwiches and apples were stacked on his tail. "This is one show we can't miss!"

In a few minutes Rex came into the

lunchroom. He was carrying the sub-stitute brown bag and looking mad.

"Do you think he noticed the differ-ence?" asked Sara.

Hank made a face. "Are you kidding? He wouldn't notice if his mom turned into a pterodactyl."

Rex sat down at one end of a table of first graders. They all shrank away from him. Their eyes were wide.

He pulled out a sandwich.

He crammed it into his mouth.

He began to chew.

"YEEECHH! UGGGGH! PTOOEY!"

The whole room exploded in a roar.

Tufts of alfalfa sprouts were stuck in Rex's jagged teeth. So were green and red shreds of cabbage. And big leaves of spinach.

"Euw. Yuck," said Annette with a shudder.

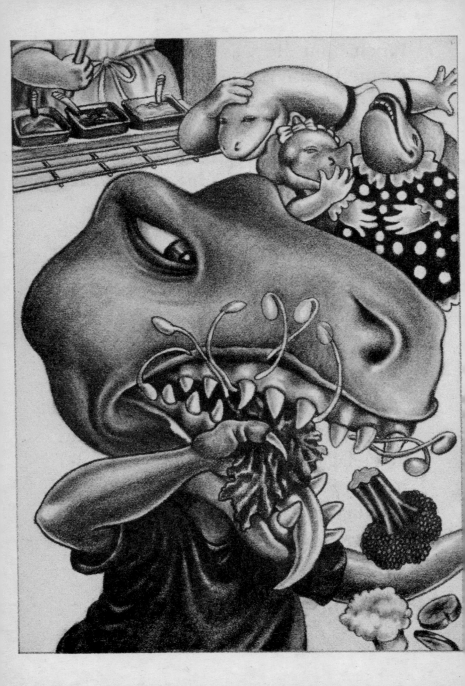

"It looks like Rex hasn't been flossing lately," observed Hank.

Rex tried to pull the shreds out of his teeth. All around him dinos were stuffing fists into their mouths so they wouldn't laugh. No one wanted to make Rex mad.

But he was already mad. Fuming.

He ripped apart all the other sandwiches.

"Turnips!" he shrieked. "Brussels sprouts! Cauliflower!"

One little first grader held out her lunch bag. "Want some granola?"

Rex pushed the bag away.

He stared at Sara and Ty and their friends. His eyes glowed an angry red.

They looked down quickly.

"I'll get whoever did this!" Rex shouted.

They pretended not to hear him.

Annette raised her head to look at the others. Her voice was low. "Mission accomplished. Now it's my turn to dare someone else."

"Later," Sara warned. "Let's not talk about it any more here. We don't want to make him suspicious."

CHAPTER
5

After school, the dinos were working on their costumes in Sara and Ty's living room. Paper, cloth, glue, scissors, and marker pens were spread out on the floor.

Ty was making a shaggy lion's mane out of old carpet.

Maggie was cutting eye holes into a white sheet. She was going to be a ghost. Maggie liked to keep her costumes simple. That way she could concentrate on the best part of Halloween: eating the treats.

Annette was going to be a rabbit. She was cutting long ears out of pink and gray paper.

Spike was making an alligator costume. He was cutting strips of green and brown felt to put on his back.

Patrick was making a big Denver Dinos design. He had an old baseball shirt to put it on.

Sara was gluing pink, white, and red streamers onto a pointed hat. Her pink fairy princess cloak was on a chair.

Hank still didn't know what he was going to be.

"Let's trick-or-treat on our street," Sara said to the others. "Like last year."

"But I only got three bags of candy here last year," protested Maggie. "Let's go to Dino Dell Acres. I hear the treats are *great* there."

"But we don't know anyone at Dino Dell Acres," said Ty. "Our parents wouldn't let us."

Sara cut the streamers off neatly. "Besides, Mom said we could have cider and doughnuts here later."

Maggie brightened. "Oh, well, in that case. . . ."

"Just as long as we stay away from Fossil Street," said Patrick with a shudder. "And Mr. Trachodon's house."

"We will," promised Sara.

"No way we're going back to that place," agreed Spike.

"Mr. Trachodon isn't our biggest problem," Hank reminded them. "It's Rex. If he figures out who was behind his lunch special, we're in big trouble."

"What's Rex going as?" asked Ty.

"Dracula," Annette answered. "He was bragging about his cloak. He's sure he'll win the prize for scariest."

"He could do that without a

costume," said Hank.

He put on Sara's princess cloak and twirled around.

"Rex should change his image. He should wear something like this."

"Hey, that's not a bad idea," Annette said.

"What do you mean?" asked Ty.

Annette was grinning. "Remember Mrs. D. said to leave our costumes backstage in the morning? It's pretty dark back there. What if someone switched a certain pink cloak with a certain black cloak?"

Sara frowned. "No. I want to wear this cloak myself." She pulled the cloak away from Hank.

"But it's my turn to dare," continued Annette. "And I *dare* you!"

"Double dare!" everyone yelled.

"All right, all right," Sara agreed at last. "Ty, you'll have to help. I think it will take two of us."

"Did you decide what to be, Hank?" asked Maggie.

Hank grabbed some pink and white streamers. Then he wound them around himself.

"A candy cane?" he asked. "Since I'm so sweet?"

"Try again, man," said Spike.

CHAPTER
6

The next morning, the Dino School auditorium was busy. Dinos were carrying costumes backstage.

There was lots of running.

There was lots of jumping off the stage.

And there was lots of shouting.

Mrs. D. was in the front row. She wore five chains of wooden pumpkins.

Mr. Pterodactyl perched nearby.

"My class, use the shelves back there," he called. "And no jumping!"

"My class, use the chairs," called Mrs. D. "And be careful in the dark."

Sara and Ty were sitting behind the teachers. They had already put their costumes in a corner backstage.

They were pretending to be just watching.

But they were really waiting for Rex.

They didn't have long to wait.

The stage curtain started trembling. The floor under their feet vibrated.

Rex came pounding down the aisle. He carried a long black cloak.

"Why, Rex," Mrs. D. said. "How nice to see you so bright and early!"

"I'm going to win!" he told her importantly. "No way I'm not!"

Rex ripped the curtains aside and disappeared. Backstage, he tripped little Diana Deinonychus. Then he bonked Hank on the head with his knuckles.

"Knucklehead," he yelled.

He went onstage. He leaped down and ran up the aisle.

Swish-thump. "Gently, Rex, gently!" Mrs. D. called.

She looked at her watch. "Time for class, everyone," she announced.

"Uh, we have to check something backstage," Ty said.

"We'll be quick," Sara promised.

When all the other dinos were gone, Ty and Sara climbed up on the stage.

Backstage was very dark. Sara made her way to the corner where she and Ty had left their costumes.

All around were shadowy lumps where other dinos had dropped their costumes.

"This is great," Ty complained. "How will we ever find—Ow!"

He had banged his knee into a chair. A long, black cloak was draped on it. A Dracula cloak!

"Here it is," he whispered. He threw

it over his arm.

Sara carried the princess cloak over from the corner. She laid it over Rex's chair. Then she and Ty tiptoed back to the corner.

Sara picked up two costumes from the floor. One was Ty's lion costume. One was a panda bear costume.

She sighed. "I still wish *I* could wear the princess cloak in the contest instead of my panda one from last year."

"You can wear the other one trick-or-treating," Ty said. He put the Dracula cloak on the floor. Then he covered it with his lion costume and Sara's panda costume.

"If you get it back in one piece, that is."

They hurried to their classroom.

Outside Room 211, noise was coming through the closed door.

They went in. Spike was balancing a tall stack of books on his tail.

The stack was wobbling.

"Two more!" Hank called. "I dare you!"

Annette and Diana were doing headstands on their desks. "I can stay up longer," Annette bragged.

"Cannot!"

"Can too!"

Sara and Ty got ready to join the fun.

Suddenly the door opened.

A huge head on a long neck snapped into the room.

It was a giraffe!

Spike dropped the books. Crash!

Diana and Annette toppled over.

All the noise stopped.

Patrick was the first to speak. "Where's our teacher?"

The giraffe was silent.

Then Sara noticed five chains made of pumpkins around the giraffe's neck.

Swish-thump! went the giraffe's tail.

The giraffe took off its mask.

It was Mrs. D.!

Then everyone started laughing.

Mrs. D. laughed, too. "Looks like I fooled you," she said. "I'm sorry. I couldn't wait for the contest."

She put a stern look on her face. "But next time if you don't behave, who knows what I'll turn into?"

"I knew it was her all the time," Rex muttered.

"Now let's get busy," said Mrs. D.

Once again, the day dragged on.

First, reading groups.

Then multiplication tables.

Then a health quiz. "How many teeth can duckbill dinos have?" asked Mrs. D.

"Two thousand," answered Annette.

"Correct," said the teacher. "So it's important to brush and floss often."

At lunchtime, the dinos noticed that Rex had two bags of sandwiches.

"Making up for yesterday," said Hank.

But at least Rex didn't look mad any more. In fact, the dinos caught him actually smiling once.

"It's because he thinks he's going to win a prize," Annette figured.

"I think he is, too," Sara said with a grin. "But maybe not the one he thinks he'll win."

Finally it was two o'clock! Dinos and teachers poured into the auditorium. Most of them sat in the audience.

Mrs. D.'s class and Mr. Pterodactyl's class went backstage. Sara and Ty slipped in right behind Rex.

It was still very dark. Now it was crowded, too. Crowded with horns and tails and scaly elbows. Forty dinos were trying to get dressed at once.

The twins dressed quickly. They could just make out Rex's shape as he put on the princess cloak.

Mr. Pterodactyl called, "Ready?"

He and Mrs. D. were at the far end of the stage. They were the judges.

The curtain was yanked open. Rex pushed some ghosts and witches and pirates aside. *He wants to be first*, Sara thought. *Just you wait, you bully*.

She heard Mr. Pterodactyl chuckle. She heard Mrs. D.'s soft laugh.

Soon everyone onstage and in the audience was laughing.

The twins dashed out of their corner. They threw Rex's Dracula cloak back on its chair. Then they melted into the crowd on the stage.

Rex was standing in front.

He was smiling.

He had Dracula fangs stuck on his teeth.

Sara's dainty pink fairy princess cloak hung down to his knees.

"Why, Rex, that's beautiful!" Mr. Pterodactyl exclaimed.

"And so amusing!" said Mrs. D.

The laughter grew louder.

Rex looked confused.

Then he looked down at himself.

His skin turned as pink as the cloak.

Wildly he looked for a way to escape. But the stage was blocked at one end by the other dinos and at the other end by the judges.

He couldn't even jump off. Ms. Brachiosaurus, the principal, was sitting right below him.

The dino friends held their sides. They choked back gasps of laughter all through the judging.

Finally Mr. Pterodactyl said, "We have the winners! And one costume is so good that it's won two prizes!"

Mr. Pterodactyl flapped over to Rex. He was wearing a Batman costume.

"For prettiest!" he said. He placed a gold crown on Rex's head.

Everyone clapped and whistled. Rex clenched his fists and ground his teeth.

Then Mrs. D. came over to him. She was wearing her giraffe mask again.

"Congratulations, Rex," she said. She held out a trophy. It read FUNNIEST.

"I'm so proud of you for being such a good sport!"

Rex glared at her. He grabbed the trophy and hid it behind his back.

The other prizes were given. Then

it was all over.

Rex bolted backstage. He threw Sara's cloak on the floor.

Then he stomped to the chair where he'd left his Dracula cloak.

It was still there.

Sara and Ty saw him scratch his head. He was trying to figure it all out.

Then he snatched the Dracula cloak and was gone.

Sara sighed with relief. "I'd better get my costume," she said.

"Let's be sure he's left," Ty warned.

The twins waited for ten minutes. Everyone else was gone. Sara packed the princess costume in a bag with the panda and lion. Then she and Ty hurried out the door.

The twins hadn't seen a pair of angry red eyes glowing behind the curtain.

But the eyes had seen them.

CHAPTER
7

"Now, take your flashlights, and stick together," Mr. Triceratops said.

"Only go to houses where you know someone," Mrs. Triceratops added.

"And don't eat *anything* until we have a chance to check it out," Mr. Triceratops reminded them.

"Okay, Dad. All right, Mom. We know." Words tumbled out of the twins' mouths. They were so excited.

All the dinos were excited tonight.

They had played two tricks on Rex.

And they were going trick-or-treating by themselves for the first time!

Last year Mrs. Triceratops had

walked with them.

That wasn't so bad.

But this was better!

Outside there were warm, friendly lights. Porch lights. Lights on fence posts. Glowing lights from grinning jack o' lanterns.

"Let's start with Mrs. Parasaurolophus," Sara said. That was their art teacher at school. She lived next door.

"Don't you all look great!" the teacher exclaimed when she opened the door. She gave them chocolate pumpkins.

"What are you, Hank? A mummy?" she asked. "Or a barber pole?"

Hank had wrapped pink and white streamers over his mouth. He shook his head.

"He can't talk," explained Annette.

"Yeah, it's a real loss," said Spike.

"He's supposed to be a candy cane."

They went to the Tarbosaurus house. Then to the Spinosauruses'. Soon they had gone to every house.

Maggie patted her bag. It was starting to bulge. "Where next?"

"Let's try Bone Road," Sara suggested. "Some people from Mom's office live there."

There was an empty lot at the corner of Bone Road.

At least it looked empty.

They started walking by.

"Did you hear something?" Sara asked Annette.

"Maybe." Her friend's voice was very soft. "Like a rustling?"

"Keep walking, guys," said Spike calmly.

They went a few more steps. They stopped again.

"Did anyone else hear a clicking sound?" asked Maggie.

"Yeah," said Ty. "Like a chain?"

"A bicycle chain!" cried Sara the detective.

A rough voice shouted, "Trick or treat, you're dead meat!"

"It's Rex!" yelled Patrick.

"He must have found out about the costume!" yelled Annette.

"Run for it!" yelled Ty.

Rex popped a wheelie out of the lot as the dinos scrambled away. His Dracula cloak billowed out as he rode.

The dinos bolted through yards and gardens where Rex couldn't go. They jumped over fences. They leaped over doghouses. Soon they had lost track of where they were.

Their costumes were falling apart. Hank's streamers were in tatters. Sara's princess cloak was dirty and torn. Maggie's sheet was long gone.

But she still clutched her candy bag.

"Where are we?" she asked.

"I think we're on—" Ty began. But he didn't get a chance to finish.

ZIM ZIM ZIM ZIM! They could hear a bike's tires moving fast!

Rex was coming right at them!

"Let's separate," said Sara.

"I'll go this way!" cried Patrick, running right toward Rex.

"Wait for me," called Spike.

"No!" Patrick called back. "I'll go myself."

He shouted at Rex. "Come on! I dare you! You can't catch me on that old heap!"

Rex yelped in anger. He hated it when anyone insulted his bike.

He screeched off after Patrick.

The others raced the opposite way.

Gasping for breath, they leaned against a fence.

They waited for a minute or two.

"We have to rescue Patrick," Spike finally said. "He may be in real trouble."

"Let's go!" Sara cried. She was shaking.

The dinos headed back the way Patrick had run. In a minute they saw something lying on the sidewalk.

"It's Patrick's baseball cap," said Spike. He hung it gently on his spikes.

"We'd better hurry," said Sara.

They found themselves on the corner of Fossil Street. The street was almost pitch black. Only one dim streetlight was shining.

"Look!" Annette exclaimed.

Patrick was crouched on the front

porch of Mr. Trachodon's house. The house looked even spookier in the dark. One faint light shone through the shaded front window.

The dinos could see Rex halfway down the street. He was pedaling slowly, looking carefully around.

"Patrick picked a great place to hide," Hank muttered.

Sara leaned out to see better.

"Careful!" Ty tried to pull her back. "You're right under the streetlight."

But it was too late. Rex had seen her.

With a roar he headed for the group.

At the same time they heard a crash. They saw Patrick sprawled on the porch. His back end was in the air.

The door to the house was open. Patrick's long tail was still outside. The rest of him was inside.

The dinos threw themselves across

the street. They dodged Rex and dashed up onto the porch.

Patrick was struggling to get up.

His friends tugged on his tail to pull him out.

Someone else pulled him in.

Then they all crashed inside the house together.

The door slammed.

Outside, Rex waited by the hedge.

CHAPTER
8

The first thing the dinos noticed was the smell. It was a good smell. Cinnamon and apples.

The next thing they noticed was a very old lady dino sitting in a rocker. She was bundled up in a quilt. She was stroking a sabre-toothed kitten.

And the third thing was Mr. Trachodon himself.

He was old.

He was bald.

He was dragging a huge sack toward them.

Closer. Closer.

"Mama and I have waited so long," he said.

The dinos huddled together. Sara gasped. Annette shivered.

Mr. Trachodon pulled the sack in front of him. He opened up the top. He reached in. What was he going to do to them?

Patrick closed his eyes. Ty took a deep breath. Sara got ready to scream.

Then Mr. Trachodon pulled some gigantic candy bars out of the bag.

He was smiling.

"Every year I make spiced cider and buy candy. But nobody comes trick-or-treating here. I end up throwing all the candy away. But not tonight! You're my first trick-or-treaters ever."

Maggie recovered first. "You've been throwing candy away?" she asked in horror. She grabbed five bars and stuck them in her bag.

Patrick cleared his throat. "Uh, Mr.

Trachodon, I'm sorry, but we weren't trick-or-treating.   I was hiding."

"From someone who's still outside," Sara added.

Mr. Trachodon looked sad. "I thought it was too good to be true."

Hank spoke up. "Well, no offense, but your house *is* kind of scary-looking."

The old dino sighed. "I have a bad back. It's hard for me to keep up."

"But what about the shadows?" Spike asked.

"Shadows?" Mr. Trachodon said. "Oh! You mean these?"

He turned so that his side faced the window. He rolled up his sleeves.

He fluttered his fingers and made swoops with his hands. Dark shapes flew around on the shade.

"Birds!" cried Patrick.

Mr. Trachodon placed one hand over the other. He wiggled his fingers.

"A spider!" shouted Annette.

"This is what we saw on Saturday," said Sara.

A high-pitched cackle from the rocker made them jump.

"And that's what we heard on Saturday," Ty said.

"Don't mind Mama," Mr. Trachodon told them. "She just loves this. We hardly ever go out. This is her only entertainment."

Mr. Trachodon made a swinging monkey. Two elephants. A rooster.

"I wonder if Rex is enjoying the show," said Ty.

"I was wondering the same thing," said Sara. "And that gives me an idea."

She whispered something to Mr. Trachodon. He concentrated for a minute. Then he started giving the dinos directions.

"You stand here," he told Hank. "Now you get behind him." He pointed to Annette. "Now you in front. . . . That's right. . . . Bring that tail over. . . . Watch the horns. . . . There!"

The seven dinos were all bunched together. They made one solid shape. Like a statue.

"Now stand in front of the window."

The dinos inched their way over, still connected.

Mr. Trachodon moved the lamp so the light was just right.

"Wave your arms and tails," he said. "Shake your heads a little, too."

They did as they were told.

Old Mrs. Trachodon laughed and laughed. Her rocker was going a mile a minute.

Outside they heard a loud yell.

And no wonder. On the other side of the shade, all Rex could see was the twitching, quivering form of a seven-headed, seven-tailed monster with spikes, horns, a club, and a lion's mane!

After the yell came another sound.

The ZOOM of a bike being ridden away at top speed.

"I don't think he'll bother you for a while," Mr. Trachodon said.

Mr. Trachodon gave the dinos the rest of the candy bars. He gave Sara and Ty some cider to take home.

"Now be sure to come back next Halloween," he said.

"We will," Sara said. "Thanks!"

They ran down the street.

Spike handed Patrick his Denver Dinos cap. "Why didn't you let me go with you?" he asked.

Patrick put on the cap.

"Well, I was the one who made Rex mad in the first place. And I didn't like being called chicken, either."

"I'm sorry I called you a chicken, Patrick," Annette said. "You were braver than anyone."

"Annette's right," Sara said, smiling at Patrick. "You were brave."

"So the mystery of Mr. Trachodon's house is finally solved," Ty said.

Sara looked down at her ruined cloak. "Yes. Now the only mystery is: How will we explain these wrecked costumes to Mom?"

CHAPTER
9

The next day the dinos were playing in the schoolyard before the bell. As usual.

Patrick was looking at baseball cards. As usual.

Spike and Hank had a hot game of Heads and Tailsies going. As usual.

Rex rode in on his bike. As usual.

He didn't try to run them down.

That was not usual.

They watched as he parked his bike and walked quietly into school.

They watched as he sat quietly all morning.

They watched as he quietly ate his lunch.

Finally they couldn't stand it any more.

"This is no fun!" said Hank. "I want the mean, nasty old Rex back!"

"Me, too," said Ty.

"I know!" Hank pulled something out of his pocket. All the other dinos grinned and nodded.

After school they hid behind the bleachers.

They watched Rex get on his bike.

They watched him ride down the driveway.

Then they heard the other dinos in the playground begin to laugh and call out.

"Hey, some decoration!"

"Rex looks so pretty in pink!"

"Matches his pretty pink cape!"

Pink streamers were flying out behind Rex. Hank had glued them under Rex's bike seat.

Rex heard the laughter.

He looked back and saw the streamers.

With a shout, he ripped them off and flung them away.

He saw the dino friends by the bleachers.

"I'm gonna get you guys!" he yelled. "You're history!"

In a second he was racing toward them.

"Hold onto your hats!" cried Patrick. He held his Denver Dinos cap down firmly.

They all dived for cover.

"Now, that's more like it!" said Hank.

Be sure to read the next Dino School book,
Battle of the Class Clowns